An I Can Read Book™

LITTLE WOLF
BIG WOLF

MATT NOVAK

HarperCollinsPublishers

To Anne Hoppe,
for her patience and tireless devotion
to wolves (and authors)
of all sizes.

HarperCollins®, 🐾®, and I Can Read Book®
are trademarks of HarperCollins Publishers Inc.

Little Wolf, Big Wolf
Copyright © 2000 by Matt Novak
Printed in the U.S.A. All rights reserved.

Library of Congress Cataloging-in-Publication Data
Novak, Matt.
  Little Wolf, Big Wolf / story and pictures by Matt Novak.
     p.   cm. — (An I can read book)
  Summary: Although they are very different, two wolves discover that they can still be friends.
  ISBN 0-06-027486-7. — ISBN 0-06-027487-5 (lib. bdg.)
  [1. Wolves—Fiction. 2. Friendship—Fiction.] I. Title. II. Series.
PZ7.N867Li   2000   99-10610
                                                                          CIP
                                                                           AC

1   2   3   4   5   6   7   8   9   10
❖
First Edition
www.harperchildrens.com

CONTENTS

NEW FRIENDS

One day

Little Wolf was picking daisies

in the forest.

There he met a wolf named Big Wolf.

"I love daisies," said Big Wolf.

"Me too!" said Little Wolf.

"We are so alike!

I am sure we will be best friends."

"I am sure too," said Big Wolf.

"Daisies smell so pretty,"

Little Wolf said.

"I don't know about that,"

said Big Wolf,

"but they sure do taste good."

He ate up all the daisies.

"Ugh," said Little Wolf.

"Maybe we are not so alike."

"I like sticks," said Big Wolf.

"So do I!" said Little Wolf.

"Great!" said Big Wolf.

"Sticks make terrific toothpicks."

"Toothpicks?" Little Wolf asked.

"I use sticks to make baskets.

I guess we're kind of different."

"I like stones," Big Wolf said.

"Do you like stones?"

"I love stones!" said Little Wolf.

"I am so glad," said Big Wolf.

"Me too," Little Wolf said.

"I collect funny-shaped stones
and paint faces on them."

"Sounds like a lot of work to me," said Big Wolf.

"I skip them across the pond."

"We aren't alike at all, are we?" asked Little Wolf.

"We are very different," said Big Wolf.

11

The two wolves sat by the pond.

Splish! Splish! Splunk!

went Big Wolf's stones.

After a while Little Wolf said,

"That looks like fun.

Is it hard to do?"

"A little," said Big Wolf,

"but I could show you how."

"I would like that,"

said Little Wolf.

"We will need more stones,"
Big Wolf said.

"We can collect some
and put them in my basket,"
said Little Wolf.

"I like your basket,"
said Big Wolf.

"Was it hard to make?"

"A little," said Little Wolf,
"but I could show you how."

"I would like that,"
said Big Wolf.

"All we need is more sticks,"

Little Wolf said.

"We both know where to find those,"

said Big Wolf.

And the two best friends went off

to collect sticks and stones together.

THE VISITOR

Little Wolf opened

his newspaper.

At the top it said,

WARM AND SUNNY TODAY.

"Hooray!" Little Wolf said.

"It is the perfect day

for Big Wolf's visit."

19

Then Little Wolf saw something
at the bottom of the page.
It said, A CLEAN HOUSE
MAKES YOUR VISITOR
FEEL RIGHT AT HOME.
CALL BUSY BEAR
CLEANING SERVICE TODAY.

"I do want Big Wolf

to feel right at home,"

said Little Wolf,

so he called

Busy Bear Cleaning Service.

Busy Bear came right over.

"What a mess!" she said.

She washed Little Wolf's clothes

and put them away.

"Don't wear these again,"

she said.

Busy Bear fluffed the sofa.

"Don't sit here," she said.

She washed the dishes.

"Don't use these," she said.

She mopped the floor until it shined.

"Don't walk on this," she said.

25

Little Wolf looked around

his neat, clean house.

"Now Big Wolf will feel at home,"

he said.

"Remember! Don't touch a thing,"

said Busy Bear as she left.

Little Wolf stood very still

and waited . . .

and waited.

Knock! Knock! Knock!

Little Wolf tiptoed over

and opened the door.

"Hello, Big Wolf," said Little Wolf.

"Hello, Little Wolf," said Big Wolf.

Big Wolf threw his coat on the floor
and his hat on the lamp.

"Oh, no," said Little Wolf.

Big Wolf tracked mud

right across the clean floor.

"Oh, no! Oh, no!" said Little Wolf.

Big Wolf tossed his big suitcase

onto the table.

Dishes crashed to the floor.

"Yikes!" cried Little Wolf.

Then Big Wolf plopped down

and flattened all the sofa cushions.

31

Big Wolf looked around.

He saw clothes everywhere.

He saw the muddy floor,

and the smashed dishes,

and the rumpled sofa.

"What a mess!" he said.

"It's all ruined!" Little Wolf cried.

"Now you'll never feel at home!"

"But I do feel at home,"
said Big Wolf.
"You do?" Little Wolf asked.
"Yes," Big Wolf said.
"Your house is nice and messy,
just like mine.
I feel right at home."
"Oh," said Little Wolf.
"I'm glad you feel that way."
He plopped down on the sofa.
"Now I feel right at home too."

A FUN PARTY

"Let's have a party,"

Little Wolf said to Big Wolf.

"I will go invite my friends,

and we will have lots of fun."

"I will get food for the party,"

said Big Wolf.

"We can't have fun

if we are hungry."

He took a big sack

and went into the forest.

Big Wolf saw a chicken.

"Yummy," he said.

He tossed the chicken into the sack.

Next Big Wolf saw a rabbit.

"Tasty," he said.

He tossed the rabbit into the sack.

Then Big Wolf saw a pig.

"Jackpot," he said.

Big Wolf smacked his lips.

He tossed the pig into the sack.

"This will make a fun party,"
said Big Wolf.

He skipped back to
Little Wolf's house.

But when he got there,

Little Wolf was crying.

"What is wrong?" asked Big Wolf.

"I did not find any of my friends,"

Little Wolf said.

"We cannot have the party!"

"That is too bad," said Big Wolf,

"but you will feel better

when you see all the good things

I have in my sack."

Big Wolf dumped out the sack.

"What a wonderful surprise!"

Little Wolf shouted.

"I'm glad you like it,"

said Big Wolf.

He licked his lips.

"You invited all my friends

to our party," said Little Wolf.

"Friends?" asked Big Wolf.

"Party?" asked the pig.

"I'm glad you have all met Big Wolf,"
Little Wolf said.

"This will be a great party!"

They played hide-and-seek
and pin the tail on the donkey.
They sang from the rooftop
and danced in the forest.
They all had so much fun,
everyone, even Big Wolf,
forgot to be hungry.